A FORGE YOUR FREAKY FATE BOOK

BETRAYAL &
BLACK LACE

Written by BRET NELSON

Based on Characters Created by STEVEN KOSTANSKI

Illustrated by STEW MILLER

Encyclopocalypse Publications
www.encyclopocalypse.com

An Encyclopocalypse Book

Copyright © 2026 by Steven Kostanski and Mark Alan Miller.

All rights reserved.

Based on characters from the motion picture *Frankie Freaeko*.

Cover design by Amanda Dempsey.

Interior layout and design by Mark Alan Miller.

First Encyclopocalypse paperback edition, 2026.

Printed in the United States of America.

ISBN: 978-1-966037-65-1

No part of this publication may be reproduced, stored in a retrieval system, or transmitted in any form or by any means (electronic, mechanical, photocopying, recording, or otherwise) without the prior written permission of the publisher.

A FORGE YOUR FREAKY FATE BOOK

BETRAYAL & BLACK LACE

Foreword

As I continue my relentless effort to craft the most obscure cross-media promotions for my films, I proudly present to you this sultry spinoff of my hit film Frankie Freako. It's an erotic thriller "forge-your-freaky-fate" adventure, starring Frankie Freako's lifelong pal and tech wizard Boink.

I won't spoil the plot here, but I can tell you it's packed with excitement and suspense, thanks to the masterful storytelling of literary powerhouse Bret Nelson. This masterpiece belongs in a museum, but through some twist of freaky fate, this book (and Boink's destiny) now lies in your hands.

Shabadon't let him down!

SKostanski

-Steve Kostanski

6

"I feel like I can tell you anything," says Roberta.

"Shabadoo," you reply. And that's exactly what she needed to hear.

She confides in you, saying the reason she spends so much time with Jacked is that Wade doesn't trust her. She didn't hire this trainer. Wade did, to spy on her. To eat her time so it won't be spent anywhere else. Jacked isn't her lover (like everyone thinks). He is her jailer.

She spends a great deal of time isolated in her hobby hut, next to the pool house. There, she follows her true passion: Pogs. She has thousands of them. Hundreds of slammers as well.

Share more with Roberta (turn to 77)

or

End the conversation and
keep things businesslike (turn to 47)

7

You are accused and it's gotta be a frame up. Time to make a choice.

Maybe you should lay low and
see what happens (turn to 46)

or

You can turn yourself in. After all,
you've done nothing wrong (turn to 89)

or

Dig around for information that
will prove your innocence (turn to 49)

8

Holly Nicollette is a terrible lawyer. The judge disbars her, and you are sentenced to life in prison.

She doesn't return your calls. After a time, you hear that she's moved to California's wine country to open a bed and breakfast with her husband of 15 years.

You didn't know she was married.

You spend the next 48 years digging a tunnel in the wall behind your bunk. The stone and packed earth are unyielding but with patience and an unlimited supply of acidic ketchup packets and plastic spoons from the commissary, you finally break through to the sewer system.

You crawl to freedom through five hundred yards of shit-smelling foulness you can't even imagine, or maybe you just don't want to. Five hundred yards... that's the length of five football fields, just shy of half a mile.

Once you make it to the river and get cleaned up, you feel odd. Two days later, you have died of dysentery.

THE END

10

Wade Walters is dead. He's been found in the pool house restroom. There's arsenic in his system. Blunt force trauma to his head and the dent in his skull matches a pipe found at the scene with his blood on it. He's been shot three times from behind, with three different guns.

Betsy Lorenzo, the coroner, has already performed the autopsy. His death has been ruled a suicide and per Wade's wishes the body was cremated.

Call 1-800-SAD-GIFT and send flowers to Roberta
(turn to 97)
or
Something doesn't seem right. Maybe you should check out the crime scene (turn to 85)

12

"You won't call the police! They're after you!" says Jacked. Maybe he's not so dumb after all. He says he loves Roberta and believes you did it.

He says he doesn't know anything about a frame up.

(turn to 34)

14

The plexi-panel window with a view of space shows a three-second countdown as the room flashes red. At the end of the countdown, the window slides open.

Silently, you are pulled into the vacuum of space, where your corpse will drift for eons.

THE END

16

Every other evening, right before they close, Jacked Jacko goes to the Gainer's Grocery Gargantua-Mart to stock up on protein powders, nutrition bars, and meat. He always parks around back so his matte-black Charger won't get dinged.

Right on time, you see him exit the store and pile the booty into the trunk. As he's easing his booty into the driver's seat, you leap out of the darkness and confront him. He raises his fists and tells you to back off.

The spring-loaded boxing glove leaps from your backpack and bops him right in the kisser. When he comes to, you have him tied up in his own back seat. You question him. He claims to know nothing.

Try to force a confession out of him (turn to 34)
or
Threaten to call the police (turn to 12)

18

Just when you thought you were getting somewhere, the door flies off its hinges. The police have found you. You are jacked into the system with incriminating files open all over the screens.

Shabadoo.

There's no sense fighting it. You give up, and you're sentenced to a LONG STRETCH in the stony lonesome.

One morning out in the yard, while you tend the prison garden, something feels off. You see movement and hear a single footstep, but it's too late. Six inmates create a people circle around you. Your world becomes a nightmare of stomps and kicks. Just before the killing blow, you hear one of them say, "Roberta sends her regards."

They didn't even get your name right on the toe tag. It says "Joe."

Your body is cremated, and your ashes are part of a paperwork mix-up. You end up in an urn intended for a prize-winning dachshund named "Murray." You sit on a shelf in a house with people you don't know.

THE END

20

You enter the building the way you always have. When you get to the hall leading to Wade Walters' office, something is different. There is another door on the adjacent wall, to the west.

A large, metal door that's never been there. It's unlocked, so you open it. There is a long hallway beyond. So long, you can't see the end of it. How can this new door (and the long hallway beyond it) exist?

Your security systems cover every inch of the place. You are the one who installed them. The double doors facing this new one are a known quantity. They lead to the east side inventory processing room. The frosted glass door on the adjacent wall leads to Wade Walters' office

This new door should open onto the main parking area on the other side of the wall. But it doesn't.

Go outside and investigate (turn to 114)
or
Go down the long hall that shouldn't exist (turn to 64)
or
See Wade in his office and ask about this (turn to 119)

21

You dial a number on the payphone. The sketchy man working the front desk dials his phone, too. He keeps staring at you as he whispers into the mouthpiece. This feels wrong.

You hang up the payphone before the call connects and head back to your room. Through the window, you see whirling red and blue lights. A bullhorn announces they've got the building surrounded.

You go quietly (turn to 89)

22

Through a series of burner phones and dead-drop notices, you end up underneath a bridge at the appointed time. You think you're alone until a familiar voice startles you.

"Stepped in it this time, didn't you pal?"

It's Frankie. Fists are bumped. A case of Fart Cola is shared. And for just a little while, everything is okay.

Frankie says, "You can work this out, Dude. You are the smartest Freako I know, and I know EVERYBODY!"

He's right on both counts. He tells you to find out who had the most to gain with Wade out of the picture. It might be Roberta, then again you haven't really looked any further. You'd like to spend the whole night partying with Frankie, like you used to. But that has to wait. It's important to keep moving.

One more Fart. One more fist bump. And you part ways.

Go to a seedy motel under assumed name (turn to 60)
or
Sneak back into Wide Width Waders headquarters to use the computers in the server room (turn to 49)

24

You've been on Earth for years now and things are going great! Your business, SO FREAKING SAFE (SFS), is a high-tech security company. You keep buildings and homes secure with video surveillance and hack-proof computer systems.

Most of your clients are the large businesses and elite residents of Medicine Hat. The one you like best is Wade Walters' Wide Width Waders, an outdoor apparel company for the larger person. SFS runs security at their vast plant.

Wade Walters, the owner, needs a better security system at his mansion. He's been using the same network of shoebox-sized cameras hooked to an array of CRT monitors in his basement since 1973, and it's time to upgrade. Though he's nearly 100 years old, Walters is tech savvy and sharp.

Equally sharp is Roberta Walters, Wade's new young wife. She's in her late twenties and seems to be head-over-heels in love with Wade. Just ask her personal trainer/bodyguard, Jacked Jacko, with whom she shares all her thoughts and feelings.

Jacked is a recent arrival from Freakworld. He used to work as muscle for that jerk Freaklord Munch. He's not an employee of SFS, he's a freelancer that Roberta met at a modeling gig.

Though Roberta and Jacked are always together, both make it clear to anyone who asks that there's nothing going on between them.

(turn to 26)

26

Wade Walters is at the plant all day, so he puts Roberta in charge of working with you at the mansion. You spend a lot of one-on-one time with her as you oversee the installation of the new security system. Each day wires, sensors, and cameras are added, and each day Roberta gets a little closer.

Get to know Roberta (turn to 101)
or
Keep your professional distance (turn to 47)

28

You are free. It doesn't take long for you to get a wonderful job as an engineering advisor to The Future Shop. Many of the people from your computer class in prison have key positions in tech now. That meant lots of job offers, and you picked the best one.

After a time, Frankie and Dottie visit you at

your new apartment. You party. You break stuff. You fix stuff. It's like it was before. For the first time in a long time, you're happy.

"You don't know how much weight you're carrying until you put it down," says Frankie. "Once you're lighter, you wonder why you spent so much time toting it around."

"He's right, I reckon," says Dottie.

Shabadoo.

THE END

30

You find backup recordings from all the cameras at the Walters' mansion. It doesn't take long to find what you need. You roll off a small portion of video to a floppy disc.

It's not from the day of Wade's death. It's from a month before. The video shows Roberta messing with the date/time settings on the day she had you walking all around the pool house. And the mismatched date stamps will prove your innocence.

Your video shows Roberta changing one setting while you were moving around the area that would later become the crime scene. That was on February third, so the date stamp should read 02/03/1992.

But she changed the date preferences to the United Kingdom setting, so it displays the day followed by the month. With the UK setting, the stamp reads 03/02/1992.

March the second was the day of the murder. She set you up. Had it planned all along.

So, what will you do with the disc?

Take it to the police (turn to 53)
or
Meeting the police is still too risky.
They may not believe you and toss you in jail.
Confront Roberta instead (turn to 70)

32

The control system is complicated, but the inputs you've set up for the users is simple. Enable. Disable. Most of the settings function automatically, with timers or motion/proximity detectors triggering lights and recording.

Roberta says she wants to see it all work, just so she can be comfortable with the operation.

You step her through the basics of the system settings and how to use the zoom, freeze frame, and other features. You have her dial through the monitor arrays and see the views all over the property.

She is convinced there's a blind spot by the pool area restroom. She won't let it go, so you head over there. You go into the restroom, back out again, and walk around every square foot of the area as she watches on the cameras.

You return to the control room, and she says you've put her mind at ease. So much at ease that one of the spaghetti straps on her dress drifts off her shoulder.

This is getting complicated.

Use your backpack-mounted mechanical pincer to put the strap back where it goes (turn to 83)

or

Pretend not to notice (turn to 69)

34

You give Jacked Jacko a test of general knowledge. The volume of wrong answers is staggering. He even failed the questions about shapes and colors and the sounds barnyard animals make.

It's verified. He knows nothing. If Roberta is behind this, Jacked Jacko is not the Freako she'd pick for an accomplice. She's got too much to lose, and this idiot is more of a liability than an asset.

Then, police cars flood the alley. You were spotted by the employees of the exercise store.

The cuffs are tight (turn to 89)

36

You meet your super-hot defense attorney, Holly Nicolette. She shows you the evidence the police have gathered.

They have you on camera going in and out of the pool house restroom, the very room where the crime took place. And the time/date stamps on the video match up to Wade's time of death. Roberta and Jacked have alibis for the time in question.

Furthermore, Roberta Walters says you took advantage of her. Several times. She tried to break it off, but you went nuts! They've got evidence of the time you've spent with Roberta. Hotel security videos and testimony from the staff. It's a lot to take in. What will you do?

> Return to your cell, then escape and
> prove your innocence (turn to 81)
> or
> Tell Holly your side of the story. All of it.
> You want your day in court (turn to 111)

38

It only takes a week to row to Ireland. You hitch a ride on a hay wagon and make your way through the rural countryside to the plot of land owned by Walter-Agra. It's lovely. Rolling fields where sheep wander and vegetables grow. A sturdy farmhouse stands in the center. You knock on the door.

Betsy Lorenzo, former coroner, answers. She wipes her hands on a dishtowel as the smell of something good for dinner flows past her. She is speechless. A familiar voice calls from inside the house.

"Who is it dear? Is it the seed delivery?" The speaker joins her and is disappointed that you don't have seeds. The disappointed man is Wade Walters, who faked his own death to be with his recently re-discovered high school sweetheart.

He remembers you and he invites you in. "I'm sorry for everything that's happened to you," he says. He thought the suicide story would be the end of it. He'd just disappear and nobody would be harmed. He had no idea Roberta would try to frame someone for the crime.

"There are certain financial accounts she wasn't be able to access. Life insurance and such that gets locked up in case of a suicide," he explains. "She got greedy. Needed another cause of death."

At least you have closure.

Return to The Tangy Bung (turn to 63)
or
Call the authorities to clear your name (turn to 105)

40

You check in under an assumed name at the Stinky 8 Hotel. There is no pool here. There isn't any heat or air conditioning, either. But there is a dead raccoon ripening in the parking lot.

Using the phone line to create computer connections, you hack into the case files at the police station with your Thinkpad 700. It's clumsy, but you make it work.

They have a dated, timestamped security recording of you entering the pool house restroom on the day

and time that Wade Walters was killed. But that isn't true. The only day you went in there was weeks ago. It was the day you were showing the system to Roberta.

You need to find the original recording to prove that the one the police have is a fake.

Maybe that idiot Jacked Jacko will bend to pressure. You know his movements. You've got his number.

Wait for Jacko behind exercise store (turn to 16)
or
Use the payphone in the lobby
to call Jacked Jacko
(turn to 91)

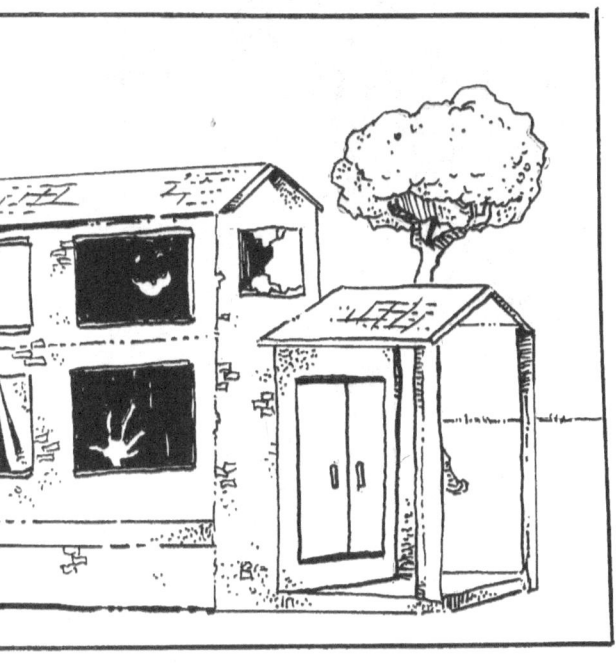

The only way to access the information you need is to send an avatar into the system's mainframe and fight the impassable security protocols you've

created.

There is a serial port in the back of your skull augment built for this purpose.

It's dangerous. You know this works with Freak Tech but you haven't tried it on Earth.

Accept the risk and go inside the system (turn to 103)
or
See if you can hack in another way (turn to 18)

44

Time to confront Roberta with the video on the floppy disc.

"Shabadoo," you say.

Jacked Jacko steps out of his hiding place in the room. "What disc?" he asks. He holds a Beretta 92 and it's pointed right at your chest. Roberta pulls an identical gun from her Fendi bag.

"These guns aren't traceable, and we can't both miss," she says. "Now what the hell are you talking about?"

"Shabadoo," you reply. You strike some keys and show them the video of Roberta tampering with the surveillance equipment.

"Do the police have this?" says Jacked. He shouts at Roberta. "What are we going to do now? He knows everything. He knows you faked that video. He knows I killed Wade that day."

"Calm down," she says, never breaking eye contact with you. "He's lying. Trying to get some leverage. If the cops had that disc, they'd have already brought us in. They don't have it."

You can Press the F2 key (turn to 71)
or
Stare them down (turn to 95)

45

You dig out your phone and you've got lots of messages. People are calling you about a news story.

(turn to 10)

46

You're on the run - hiding from the law. There's no doubt you're their lead suspect. You've seen it on all the news channels. New evidence points to you, and now you need time to think, and maybe a little help. Decisions decisions.

Hole up in a fleabag hotel
and come up with a plan (turn to 40)
or
Ambush Jacked Jacko behind the exercise store tonight
and see what he knows (turn to 16)
or
Meet Frankie Freako and ask for help (turn to 22)

47

You decide to be a pro. You cite contracts and NDAs. You can't tell anyone about the guts of the system, only its operation. Even Roberta.

She doesn't let up with the flirting. This is becoming more than a business opportunity.

One day, she shoves you into the pool house while Jacked is out buying more Squeezable Protein Slurry (BULK IN A TUBE! ™) from the exercise store.

Is it time to give in? (turn to 77)
or
Tell her how the system works (turn to 32)

49

Under cover of night, you enter Wade Walters' Wide Width Waders headquarters. There's a blind spot in the security camera grid that you always meant to fix. Now you're glad you didn't.

Inside, you move through the dim hallways and glide into the place you should have visited to begin with - the main server room. For the first time since this began, you feel safe. The wires and blinking lights are a comfort. They don't lie. They don't judge. They don't want.

But they *do* listen, and they do what you ask them to.

You pull the serial connector from you backpack, jack it into the mainframe, and take your position behind the main workstation.

Showtime. Shabadoo.

The 486 processors have blinding speed. You drill through firewalls and leapfrog over weak passwords (D-R-O-W-S-S-A-P… *really*?). Where should you start the hunt?

Look for your case folder
at the police precinct (turn to 87)

or

Check Roberta's bank and phone records (turn to 113)

  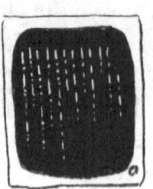

51

Success! The virtual pathways are open to you. You pop your avatar like a digital soap bubble and return to the work station in the server room.

Someone has been monkeying with the system files here. There are a few pieces you don't recognize as you look for transaction records.

In and amongst the data files, there's a program. You run it and discover it's a virtual interface that mirrors the one you've set up at the Walters' Mansion. You can access the whole system from here. But who set this up?

That's a problem for later. Right now, you've got to come up with proof that Roberta framed you.

Open the financial transaction files (turn to 11)
or
Explore the virtual interface (turn to 30)

53

The police look at the video on the floppy disc. It's enough to clear your name. Roberta gets arrested. You go free. Your business takes off like nobody's business once word gets out that your systems proved your innocence. That's the sort of thing everyone would like to have handy, just in case. Work orders pour in. So does the money.

Years later, you and Holly Nicollette sit on the porch of your custom home. You gaze at the herons over the lake, and you've never been happier, never been more in love.

You got the girl. You got the house. You got the riches. You're the luckiest boy who ever left Freakworld.

And the police will never know you manufactured the video on that floppy disc.

You got away with murder.
Shabadoo.

THE END

54

The door opens with an audible hiss. Stale, filtered air moves to greet you. You face a small control room, similar to the security center at the Waders complex. But instead of the wall covered in computer monitors, there is a plexi-panel window with a wonderful view of space.

You are alone.

Go back the way you came (turn to 69)
or
Step into the control room (turn to 65)

55

The door you came through has reappeared.

Go through the door (turn to 82)
or
Slap the red button (turn to 14)

57

The dummies you've created work well. As you tunnel your way out of the jail, the guards never guess that you're missing because your mannequins double for your sleeping selves.

The tunneling is slow, though, and you realize more time is needed.

So, you take turns during the day. In the mornings, your cellmate tunnels while you move his replica from place to place. He does the same with your replica while you tunnel in the afternoon.

And in four days, the tunnel is complete.

You are out (turn to 49)

59

You are free. It doesn't take long for you to get a wonderful job as an engineering advisor to The Future Shop. Many of the people from your computer class in prison have key positions in tech now. That meant lots of job offers, and you picked the best one.

Years later, you and Holly Nicollette sit on the porch of your custom home. You gaze at the herons over the man-made lake, and you've never been happier, never been more in love.

You got the girl. You got the house. You got the riches. You're the happiest boy who ever left Freakworld.

Shabadoo.

THE END

60

You head to your room. Through the window, you see whirling red and blue lights. A bullhorn announces they've got the building surrounded.

You go quietly (turn to 89)

61

Your cellmate works in the prison barbershop. He hatches a plan to pocket some of the hair he's cut and use it to escape.

You work in the prison's mannequin shop, creating hyperrealistic figures for use in store windows. If you can steal a pair of them and outfit them with hair from the barber shop, they could take your places in the bunks while you two make your escape.

Join in the plan (turn to 57)
or
Report your cellmate (turn to 67)

62

Dottie gives you the name of a bar on Prince Edward Island and the name of someone to meet there. You can get there by car without being discovered, but it will take days.

Get a car and head out (turn to 79)
or
Hack the servers at Wide Width Waders instead (turn to 42)

The Tangy Bung feels like home. You quickly get used to this new life on the seas. Sailing and theft and pillaging are second nature to you. The devices (mechanical pincers, extended bop gloves, etc.) in your backpack make you an invaluable member of the crew.

You're a pirate now. Your ocular augment means you'll never need an eye patch.

Yar. Shabadoo.

THE END

64

You step into the featureless metal hallway. Your scanners can't penetrate the strange walls.

The door closes behind you. It's looks like a different door on this side, something you hadn't noticed before. It means doors can't be trusted here.

Follow the strange hallway (turn to 82)
or
Go back through the door (turn to 54)

65

As soon as you are clear of the doorway, it hisses shut and disappears. The wall is seamless. Gravity is stable, you don't feel lighter or heavier.

You have air to breath. There is a control panel with blinking lights and a pair of beckoning buttons.

You can't tell what it's intended to do.

Slap the big red button (turn to 14)
or
Slap the big purple button (turn to 55)

67

You find a guard in the mess hall and tell him about the escape plan, hoping this good deed might help you get an early release. He says to follow him to the warden's office. You move through the halls with the guard. Eventually, you reach a door. He holds it open for you. You go in. This door leads to a storage room. The guard isn't what he seems.

You see movement and hear a single footstep, but it's too late. The shiv is made of scrap wire (from the chain-link fence in the yard) wrapped around a bit of wood. There's not much to it, but with enough force and repetition it does the job.

As you fade away, you hear him say, "Roberta sends her regards."

They don't even get your name right on the toe tag. It says "Biff Barfdude."

Your body is donated to a medical school. Some students steal it and use it in a fraternity prank that scars a freshman's mind and turns him into a serial killer.

THE END

69 (nice)

One day, Roberta wants to get off campus and invites you along. This is the night that Jacked goes to the exercise store and he's usually gone for hours. Even with the new security system she'd rather not be alone.

You go to a hotel restaurant. It's fancy, with brass and glass accents all around. You've never shared a meal with Roberta, and you find her captivating. She takes the tiniest bites. She really knows her way around a wine list. You both get tipsy. She says driving is probably a bad idea. Good thing she has a room booked.

"There's two beds, Mr. Bardo," she says. "I'll behave, I promise."

Arriving at the room, you discover she lied. There's only one bed. She also lied about behaving.

You do the shabadoo.

This is bad, maybe you should
come clean with Wade (turn to 20)

or

Then again, why trouble the old guy? This will never happen again (turn to 83)

70

Just when you were wondering how you'd get Roberta to see you, she reaches out and asks for a meet. She knows you've been poking around the banking files. There's a lot of secret accounts she can't access. She needs your hacking help.

In exchange for getting her past the virtual security, she'll use her super-evil backup plan to get the police off your back. In addition to everything she's got on you, she's *also* got enough evidence to pin the whole thing on Jacked Jacko.

She says if you get her into the secret accounts, she'll hand over everything about Jacked to the cops. You'll be free.

Set up the meet (turn to 107)

or

Go to the cops with what *you* have (turn to 53)

71

Like a cobra striking its prey, your hand flashes across the keyboard and you strike the F2 key.

"Stop that," says Roberta, training her Beretta on your head. From her bag, the mobile phone rings. "Keep him covered," she says. Jacked Jacko gets closer and presses his gun to your chest.

Roberta lifts the phone to her ear. "Hello? Slow down. Henri, you're talking too fast. What do you mean?" Her eyes narrow and drill through you. "I understand. I'll deal with it." She drops the phone back in her bag.

"What's happening?" asks Jacked.

"Tell him, you clever little troll," says Roberta. "Shabadoo."

"Yes," says Roberta. "I don't know how, but he's put a lock on the transferred funds. Encryptions Henri can't break."

"What's happening?" asks Jacked.

"He's tied up the money, you idiot," says Roberta. "We'll have to beat the passcodes out of him." She keeps her gun trained on you.

Jacked Jacko grins. "Sounds GREAT," he says, ready to pound on your face.

(Continued next page)

Gunfire pierces the night. A pair of twin Smith & Wesson revolvers have each fired a single shot. Jacked and Roberta look confused as the Beretta 92 pistols fly from their injured hands.

Dottie steps out from the shadows, spins her smoking guns, then aims at the two culprits again. "Tarnation," she says. "What a couple of screw-tail jackasses you guys turned out to be."

"Shabadoo."

"Reach for the sky, you varmints," says Dottie. Roberta and Jacked raise their hands.

Dottie leans over and speaks to your eye augment. "Didja git all that, Frankie?"

In a van down in the parking lot, Frankie plays back the recording he just made, sourced through your eye augment. It shows Roberta and Jacked confessing to Wade Walters' murder and attempting to kill you.

"Got it all," says Frankie. His voice comes through the speaker implant just above your ear. "Let's call the fuzz. They can watch this video down here in the party wagon and clean up this mess."

"Shabadoo."

THE END

73

Just when you thought you were getting somewhere, the door flies off its hinges. The police have found you. You are jacked into the system with incriminating files open all over the screens.

Shaba-d'oh.

There's no sense fighting it. You give up, and you're sentenced to a *long* stretch in the stony lonesome.

In the years that follow, you establish a computer sciences training program at the prison. Many who served their time find good jobs on the outside, thanks to you. The program does so much good that you are granted parole.

An early release. You are free.

Enjoy your new life (turn to 59)

or

Resume the investigation (turn to 100)

There's a lot of boarding and taking and acquisitions over the next few months, but true to his word Porkfat Wobblegut is getting you closer and closer to the Emerald Isle.

Still, the real dangers of death or incarceration make themselves known each day. You consider going it alone…

> Take a lifeboat in the middle of the night
> and row to Ireland (turn to 38)
> or
> Stay aboard and stay the course (turn to 63)

77

The control system is complicated, but the inputs you've set up for the users is simple. Enable. Disable. Most of the settings function automatically, with timers or motion/proximity detectors triggering lights and recording.

Roberta says she wants to see it all work, just so she can be comfortable with the operation.

You step her through the basics of the system settings and how to use the zoom, freeze frame, and other features. You have her dial through the monitor arrays and see the views all over the property.

She is convinced there's a blind spot by the pool area restroom. She won't let it go, so you head over there. You go into the restroom, back out again, and walk around every square foot over there as she watches on the cameras. She feels better.

A few weeks later, the work is done. Roberta collapses in your arms as you leave. She's been dreaming of this moment for so long, and she begs you not to pull away.

What's a Freako to do? She's in charge, after all. You do the shabadoo.

This is bad. Maybe you should
come clean with Wade (turn to 99)

or

Then again, he doesn't really need to know.
This was just a one-time thing (turn to 69)

79

After a series of bad meals and bad slumbers in a Nissan so old that it's a Datsun, you arrive at the bar on Prince Edward Island. It's called *The Pelican's Pecker,* and it's the seediest place you've ever been in.

You meet Dottie's friend, Captain Porkfat Wobblegut. A sailor. His ship, *The Tangy Bung,* makes voyages all over the Labrador Sea and the Atlantic Ocean. He calls them "missions of spontaneous acquisition." The authorities call that "piracy."

And if you are willing to sign on as part of his lusty crew, he'll have you dropped safely on the Irish Coast in two months. And no one will be the wiser.

This sounds terrible. Head back home and hack the servers at Wide Width Waders instead (turn to 42)

or

Sign the book (turn to 75)

81

Your cellmate isn't what he seems.

You see movement and hear a single footstep, but it's too late. The shiv is made of a four-inch glass shard, reenforced with a bit of chicken wire and wrapped with duct tape for a handle. There's not much to it, but with enough repetition it does the job.

As you fade away, you hear him say, "Roberta sends her regards."

They didn't even get your name right on the toe tag. It says "Bork Blammo."

Nobody claims your body.

You rot in Potter's Field.

THE END

82

The featureless metal hallway stretches on. After quite a while walking it, you reach a door identical to the one you came though. Can you trust this door?

>Go through this door (turn to 20)
>or
>Go back the way you came
>through the first door (turn to 54)

83

As the days pass, you can't stop thinking about Roberta. Then she calls because she's having trouble with the security lights. They're on a timer but they haven't switched on tonight. She'd like you to come and check on it.

When you arrive, the lights are working fine. Roberta, in the pool for a night swim, says they just turned on. You can't find any faults in the system. By way of apology for wasting your time, Roberta asks you to join her in the pool. You don't have a bathing suit.

Turns out, you don't need one.

Shabadoo.

But you can't get over the guilt.

Wade Walters is a good man, and sooner or later you'll have to come clean with him (turn to 99)

85

You arrive at the mansion just as you have so many other days over the last few months, but it's different. Police cars are everywhere with their candy-colored lights swirling. Miles of caution tape festoon the property and uniformed officers block you from going past the driveway.

One of the detectives spots you. "Hey!" he calls. "Boink? You're Boink Bardo, aren't you? Can we have a word please?"

Talk to the detective (turn to 89)
or
Shaba-DON'T say a word and
get out of there (turn to 46)

87

The police haven't added much evidence to your top-level case file. Just a few more interviews with people who knew Wade Walters.

But while you're poking around the computer storage, you find packs of data hidden deeper on the local drives. You can crack them open, but you may be detected.

>Leave it alone and look into
>Roberta's bank records (turn to 113)
>or
>Take the deeper dive (turn to 42)

89

You get booked. Mug shots, fingerprints, faded orange jumpsuit - the works. Something about new evidence. They don't take you to a cell, they take you to an interrogation room.

>Ask for a lawyer (turn to 36)
>or
>Keep your mouth shut (turn to 4)

91

The desk clerk keeps eyeing you as you thumb quarters into the smelly payphone in the lobby. Maybe he's recognized you from the news. Or maybe he looks at everyone this way.

Ignore him and make your call (turn to 21)
or
Hang up the phone and head out the door (turn to 16)

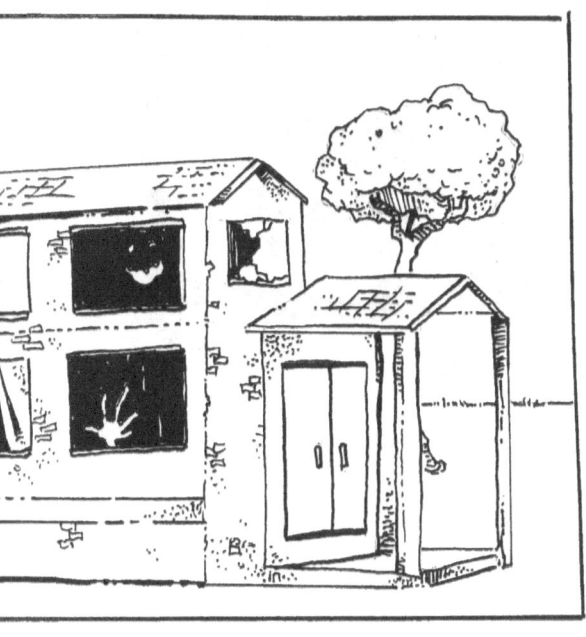

93

Roberta speaks into her mobile phone. "You're certain, all five accounts? Good. Thank you very much, Henri."

She drops the phone into her Fendi bag as Jacked Jacko walks into the room. She gives him a kiss then looks back to you. "Did you really think I'd turn on him?" asks Roberta.

Jacked holds a Beretta 92 and it's pointed right at your chest. Roberta pulls an identical gun from her bag. "These pistols aren't traceable, and we can't both miss."

"Shabadoo," you reply.

"What floppy disc?" asks Jacked. You strike some keys and show them the evidence you've gathered. The video of Roberta tampering with the surveillance equipment.

"And the police have this?" says Jacked. He shouts at Roberta. "What are we going to do now? He knows everything. He knows you faked that video. He knows I killed Wade that day."

"Calm down," she says, never breaking eye contact with you. "He's lying. Trying to get leverage. If the cops had that disc, they'd have already brought us in. They don't have it."

You can press the F2 key (turn to 71)
or
Stare them down (turn to 95)

95

The sound of gunfire pierces the night. A pair of twin Smith & Wesson revolvers have fired three shots each. Jacked and Roberta look confused as bullets tear into them. Jacked drops his gun. Roberta drops to the ground.

Jacked touches his forehead, then looks at the blood on his fingertip. The source is a black and red hole just above his left brow, still smoking. His eyes drift and he falls dead.

You run to Roberta. She takes a breath, ready to share her last thoughts with you, but the bullets rattling inside her lungs cut the speech short. She perishes looking at you.

Dottie steps out from the shadows and spins her pistols back into their holsters. "Tarnation," she says. "What a pair of tater-brained goobers they turned out to be."

"Shabadoo."

Dottie looks into your eye augment. "Did you git all that, Frankie?"

In a van down in the parking lot, Frankie plays back the recording he just made, sourced through your eye. It shows Roberta and Jacked confessing to Wade Walters' murder and attempting to kill you.

"Got it all," says Frankie. His voice comes through the speaker implant just above your ear. "Let's call the fuzz!"

"Shabadoo."

THE END

97

As you order the "SORRY YOUR MUCH OLDER HUSBAND DIED" bouquet for two-day delivery to the Walters' mansion, you see a new message on your phone - a voicemail from Frankie Freako.

> *"Hey Boink! Looks like your gravy-train wrecked. Bad news, Bardo. But you should know, one of the best subscribers to my Fun Time Phone is your chief of police. And he tells me you are IN THE FRAME. A suspect. Something about new evidence. He couldn't tell me more, but cripes, this looks bad. Your move, pal."*

Better get to the mansion and look into this (turn to 85)
or
Maybe there are bigger choices to be made (turn to 7)

99

Later, you stride through Wade Walters' Wide Width Waders headquarters. Everyone knows you here. You head for Wade's office and knock. The door swings open, but he's not there.

There's a glow coming from the desk. His computer is on, and that's unusual. He always locks the screen before he leaves.

Check the news story on the screen (turn to 10)
or
Call Wade's phone (turn to 45)

100

   In the years that passed, Roberta Walters ran Wide Width Waders at a good profit. Jacked Jacko ended up working as a trainer at hotels around the Mediterranean. Neither led extravagant lives.

   But that shell company, WalterAgra, remains a mystery. It still has holdings worldwide, but only one tangible asset: a large piece of land in Ireland. There is no information about this land anywhere. No businesses there. No address matching the coordinates.

   To discover more you'd have to go there.

   You'll violate your parole if you leave the country. Fortunately, Dottie knows some people who can help if you wish to follow this lead.

Enlist Dottie (turn to 62)
or
Let it go (turn to 28)

101

Wade's new, young wife Roberta wants to be more involved with the work you're doing.

Jacked Jacko is usually working out by the pool. He's not interested in the work you're doing because it doesn't involve dead lifts.

She wonders if the system could be tripped accidentally and how you would correct that. And if it's possible to edit the video once it's captured.

Plus, she's flirting mercilessly.

You can be polite (turn to 47)
or
Get a little closer and listen
to what she has to say (turn to 6)

103

Your avatar enters the computer system sporting an iridescent white bodysuit with dayglo trim. Your security protocols are tough indeed. Tougher than you remember them.

You battle code-bots with flying discs. You cross serial wastelands on a bicycle that leaves behind a trail of light. Finally, you reach the secret data storage columns you've been searching for.

Trouble is, there are two doors.
One is made of candy (turn to 51)
One is made of nails (turn to 109)

105

You are an international fugitive and no one in authority wants to hear your story. You are sent to an Irish prison to await extradition to the United States. While you are there, you check out a copy of Stephen King's *Later* from the prison library. You are a day late returning it, enraging the library staff.

In the dead of night, the librarians find their way to your cell and gag you. They carry you through the back halls, waving the King book at you while they mock your literary tastes.

"Who even likes *Later*?" one of the librarians taunts.

"Shabadoo," you groan.

"Okay, I'll give you that. I do enjoy his prose, too. It's always like spending time with an old friend. And he's *so* good with characters, right?"

"Shaba... do?" you ask, weakly.

"No, we're still going to kill you."

They drag you to an area of new construction and wall you in behind what will become the main exercise room. It takes seven days for you to die.

With your dying breath, you vow to have your vengeance in the afterlife.

"...sha... ba... do..."

And ever since then, if a prisoner checks out a Stephen King book, they receive a letter the next day with nothing written on it. And exactly seven days after that letter's arrival, the prisoner sneezes.

Turns out, you are lousy at vengeful haunting.

THE END

107

Through a series of burner phones and dead-drop notices, you set up a meet with Roberta at the Wide Width Waders headquarters.

She is bringing the account numbers. You are supposed to use the computers in the server room to set up money transfers to her off-shore accounts.

You both arrive on time. She has a mobile phone with her, a brand-new Motorola International 3200. When the transfers are complete, she will get a confirmation call from Henri, her overseas banker.

Roberta says that after the confirmation call is received, she'll use this same phone to call the police with a new story. She'll them that she's been afraid to tell the truth - that Jacked Jacko killed Wade and set you up. He has threatened her with harm. It should be enough to clear your name.

But first, she wants the money. You take your seat at the workstation in the office.

Do as she says and make the transfers (turn to 93)
or
Confront her with your floppy disc (turn to 44)

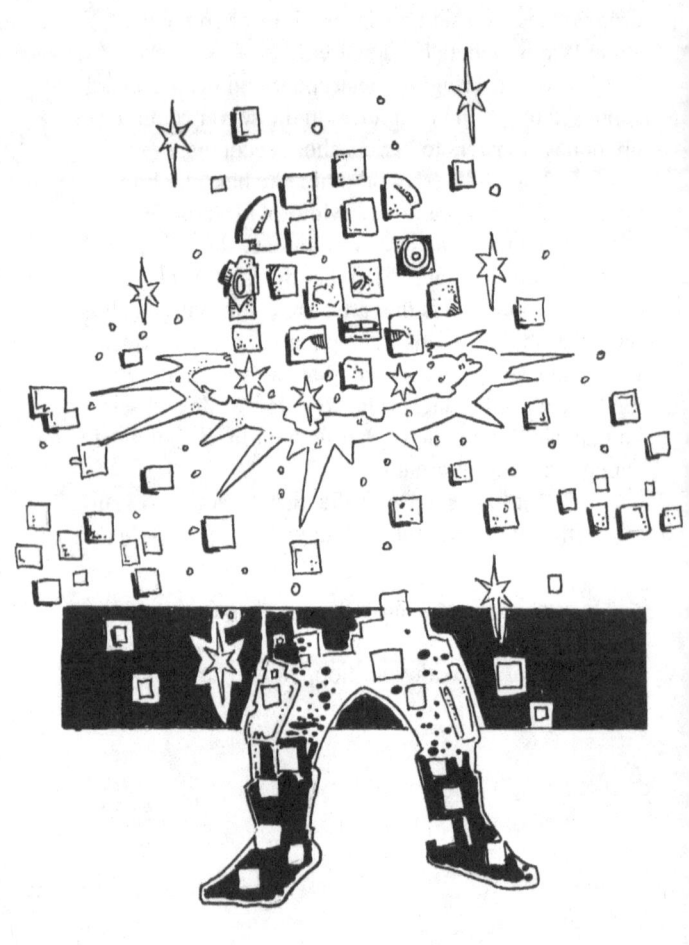

109

After several digital missteps, your avatar is no longer stable enough to exist as standalone code. You become an error string, empty of data or a soul.

You spend eternity as a digital spectre.

A ghost in the machine.

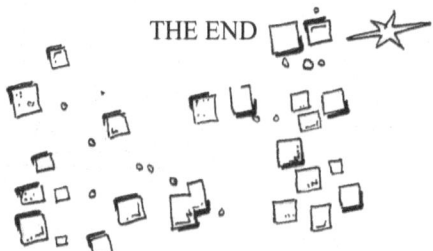

THE END

111

Super-hot defense attorney Holly Nicollette listens intently as you give your side of the story.

"Shabadoo," you say.

She puts her index finger behind the bauble on her chain necklace and mindlessly draws it left and right. "I see your point, Mr. Bardo" She leans forward and opens her briefcase. As she withdraws a legal pad and pen, the top button on her blouse comes undone.

She makes no attempt to fix it. "Tell me, when did you first meet Roberta Walters?" She clicks her pen and scribbles.

"Shabadoo," you say.

She puts down the pen and makes certain there are no cameras in this conference room. Turns out, she's freaky for Freakos. She pulls you close.

What's a Freako to do? You lean in.

She holds back a little. She's unsure what to make of your mismatched heights and skin textures. But once the piston and pearl augments in your freak stick start humming, this is all she wants from now on.

Shabadoo.

Once the clothes are back on, you discuss your case with slightly clearer heads. Holly thinks you can win this. The evidence puts you at the scene, but doesn't prove you actually did the crime. And maybe she can get Roberta to crack.

Have your day in court (turn to 8)
or
You might need more evidence,
and you can find it if you escape (turn to 61)

113

A deeper look into Wade Walters' finances brings surprising results. You were expecting to find evidence that Roberta and Jacked were siphoning all of his cash and belongings, but there's more.

Much of the money went to a shell company called WalterAgra. It has holdings worldwide, but only one tangible asset: a large piece of land in Ireland. There is no information about this land anywhere. No businesses there. No address matching the coordinates.

The only way to discover more will be to go there, but you are wanted by the police. Travel overseas will be impossible by plane or passenger ship. Fortunately, Dottie knows some people who can help if you wish to follow this lead.

Enlist Dottie (turn to 62)
or
This isn't likely to help. Forget it (turn to 73)

114

You close the door and leave the building. You get to the parking lot and examine the exterior wall where the odd door should be. It's as you thought - there is no door. No strange hallway extending into the lot, passing between the cars.

You use the scanner in your eye augment to look through the wall. There is no sign of the strange door or hallway inside.

Go back through the front door (turn to 64)
or
This is getting too weird. Maybe you should just call Wade instead (turn to 45)

THE RETRO MASS MARKET COLLECTION

COLLECT THEM ALL!

- ☐ HELLRAISER: THE TOLL
- ☐ FRIGHT NIGHT
- ☐ RE-ANIMATOR
- ☐ HARDCORE
- ☐ WISHMASTER
- ☐ HELLRAISER: BLOODLINE
- ☐ TITAN FIND
- ☐ CREATURE
- ☐ VAMP
- ☐ SCARED TO DEATH OF UNKNOWN ORIGIN
- ☐ MANBORG
- ☐ ATTACK OF THE KILLER TOMATOES
- ☐ THE SPECIAL
- ☐ TAMARA
- ☐ FORBIDDEN ZONE
- ☐ COURAGE UNDER FIRE
- ☐ LONG WEEKEND
- ☐ THE ODD JOB
- ☐ BLUE SUNSHINE
- ☐ THE ONLY HOUSE
- ☐ SQUIRM
- ☐ CRUEL JAWS
- ☐ SPLICE
- ☐ THE PIT
- ☐ THE DAY THE CLOWN CRIED
- ☐ PLAN 9 FROM OUTER SPACE
- ☐ THE TUXEDO WARRIOR
- ☐ LIFE CYCLE
- ☐ CHOPPING MALL
- ☐ ALL THROUGH THE HOUSE
- ☐ CHRISTMAS WITH THE DEAD
- ☐ VIRUS: HELL OF THE LIVING DEAD
- ☐ RATS: NIGHT OF TERROR
- ☐ MARAUDERS
- ☐ DEADGIRL
- ☐ SLEEPAWAY CAMP
- ☐ SHREDDER ORPHEUS
- ☐ SPIDER BABY
- ☐ LUST FOR A VAMPIRE
- ☐ RETURN OF THE LIVING DEAD 3
- ☑ BETRAYAL AND BLACK LACE
- ☐ SWITCHBLADE SISTERS*
- ☐ THE DEAD NEXT DOOR*
- ☐ REDNECK ZOMBIES*
- ☐ NIGHT OF THE DEMON*
- ☐ RETRIBUTION*
- ☐ OLD HENRY*
- ☐ CUBE*
- ☐ STREET TRASH*

*Coming Soon

www.ingramcontent.com/pod-product-compliance
Lightning Source LLC
LaVergne TN
LVHW032006070526
838202LV00058B/6313